FIVE GATEWAYS

| COINCIDENCE | SUBCONSCIOUSNESS | REALISATION | MYSTIC | HUMOUR |

SHREECHARAN ASHOK KUMAR

To all the events in my life which gave me the

content to write this book.

Contents

Acknowledgements

As I set my first step into the world of writing to entertain, I would first like to thank *you*, my dear readers, for believing that my works of text are worth your attention. I hope that I am worthy of that confidence and that you will not be disappointed.

Next, a big thank you to my editor: Ashok kumar Ayyappan (aka my father) who helped me in perfecting my first short stories.

Also, multiple thanks to all the authors whose books have inspired me to create one myself. I am an avid reader of detective novels (especially Sherlock Holmes and the adventures of Poirot), and mythology (like Rick Riordan's 'Percy Jackson' and 'Magnus Chase').

I

The Birthday Present

Three old women rested on royal-looking mohagony chairs, the red-colored wood looking like solid blood in the pale white light coming from the only window in the room. The rest of the room was.... Bright? Pale? Both at once? It was hard to describe.

But it was not surprising.

No. After all, the room was never made with the thought of a mortal laying his eyes on its walls.

One of the women shifted slightly. A spinning wheel sat in front of her. But it was not just another device. It was an extremely complex machine. Exactly 12 wheels spun. All of them connected. When one spun, the others did. If one stopped, the others stopped.

The wheels were spinning currently. However, the old woman wasn't stepping on the foot pedal. But the wheels spun nonetheless, allowing her to spin more yarn, slowing down when needed and speeding up when the need was raised. The woman spun her yarn in perfect coordination with the machine. But she did much more than spinning yarn. She manipulated it. She split parts of the raw fiber and made intricate braids and knots with them so fast that a mortal would have been the prey of a headache trying to follow the path of her hands.

But the knots and braids were not the same. It was not the same pattern that was ingrained upon every inch of thread. Each had a different pattern unique to itself. Just like life. But it wasn't just a comparison to life. After all, it was life itself. However, sometimes, a pattern coincided. The sign that the two holders of the lives would have their fates entangled.

But she was careful.

She did not let her hands go astray. She knew the responsibility that she had been bestowed with. One wrong twitch and the whole world might be destroyed. The Threads of Life **must** be spun correctly. Once they were made, there was no going back.

She had mastered formatting the threads of life so finely, that the word 'cloth', was named after her.

She was Clotho. The one who spins the thread of life

To her left sat another woman. Her sister. Lachesis. The allotter. She held a ball of glowing wool which, strangely, never seemed to be diminishing in size even when she drew the strings out of it, and handed it to her sister. She was careful though.

Not once did she break the line of thread that was being passed from her to her sister. If she broke it, the creation of life would have been stopped for that moment in the entire cosmos.

To the right of these two sisters sat their third sister. Atropos. The determiner of death. The complex machine had another interesting feature. It had no bobbin. Instead, the thread that came out of the wheel was collected by the 3rd sister. She took the thread and cut it at irregular intervals.

That was it. The owner of that life had his birth, the features of his life, and his death determined.

They were the 3 Fates. The 3 immortal beings who drew out the plan of life. All three of them worked in perfect sync, each's abilities complimenting the other. They did not make any mistakes in their job. With a few exceptions. Nobody is flawless. Chaos rises and evil awakens. These mistakes are not made unconsciously though. They were forced upon the threads of life by forces far more powerful than the fates.

Such an event occurs now.

Clotho's hand slowed a little. For the hundredth of a second. And started at a normal pace again. That was it. Clotho frowned. She looked at her sisters, as if to draw their attention to the scene, but they were already watching.

'Could it be ….?' Lachesis murmured as she frowned, lost in thought.

Lachesis and Clotho looked at Atropos. Or more specifically, the place where she cut the threads. Atropos looked nervous. She looked at the thread that was slowly coming out of the wheel. It was the thread that had the defect that Clotho had made. She licked her lips and lifted a shaky hand to cut the thread. But as she did so, her hand stopped mid-air. She couldn't get her hand near the thread. It was repelling it.

The life of that individual was repelling death.

Clotho closed her eyes. 'What is done is done. It cannot be revoked.' She whispered. 'Sound the alarm. Tell the gods that evil, has awakened'

🕉

A little girl sat in a chair that was too big for her, her cunning blue eyes regarding the packages wrapped in the glossy paper around her. She was in her room, but it was not like a 7-year-old's one. The walls were filled with posters, which a teenager's room would be decorated with. She hopped down and bent down to take one of her birthday presents. She spotted an insect, brutally crushed it with her heels, and smiled. Killing seemed to please her.

She unwrapped the presents one by one.

'Do you like it dear?' Her mother asked, slowly coming in through the door. The little girl looked at her mother and said in a cold, harsh voice.

'No'

'But why?'

'I WANT MORE!' she screamed.

Her mother went out of the room. A tear slid down her eyes. Ever since she could speak, her little girl, Mary had always been like this. Very violent. Always wanting more. Psychologists came and went, but there was no change in her behavior. She did not know what to do. She took a last look at the figure flinging boxes behind her back and went away.

Back in the room, Mary took the last box and shook it. A jingle betrayed the presence of metal inside. She took out from the box what seemed to be a lamp. It was not dusty, but it was old, indicated by its pale color. It had no stones embedded in it. It certainly did not look like a gift. Even a 7-year-old could see that. Mary took the box and searched for a name card. There was none. She turned her gaze back to the lamp. She started checking it thoroughly. It weighed more than it seemed to. In her inspection, she rubbed it unknowingly. That was all it took to release the substance inside. A hiss of grey gas escaped from inside and filled the room. The smoke slowly took form into the shape of a middle-aged man.

'Greetings mistress.' His voice rasped. 'Ah! it is good to be out in the open again. Thank you, ma'am.'

Mary, on the other hand, didn't look as if she was listening. Her eyes wandered over the man's body, from his solid form to his waist, where it dissolved into mist. Looking at this, the man laughed.

'Ah, yes. I see you are curious. But fear not, for I'm your slave. Ask me any three wishes, and they shall be granted. But only three, mind you. Also, You cannot wish for love, you can't kill, nor can you wish for more wishes. These are the rules of magic and so, can't be broken'

Mary was still confused, but she slowly got to her senses. After all, she was a kid. She didn't think that logically to not believe in magic.

Her mind whirred. She spoke after 10 minutes of silence, during which the semi-solid man waited patiently, inspecting his surroundings

'My first wish: I don't want the three rules to apply to me'

• 5 •

II

At 3:45

Part I

'What a beauty!'

The boy peered into the small object perched in his friend's hand. It was a swiss knife with a vibrant blue colored handle. It had Switzerland's flag's symbol on it - a white-colored plus sign surrounded by a red-colored rectangle. The rest of it was, to speak precisely, a shade of deep and translucent turquoise blue, coincidentally the same color as the sea around them. It was a work of exquisite art, which in the boy's opinion, would make any jewelry store owner jealous.

They were in a boat, in the middle of the Polperro beach. Though they were not near the coast, one couldn't say that they were just far from it either. They could see the coastline as an irregular line of sand brown and green, with a few spots of dark brown.

Both the boys lived on the coastline, in a village named Polperro, which was just about 5 dozen roads long from the coast. This automatically made the beach their sanctuary.

Their boat wasn't of an extremely good quality one. Anybody could see that. It had been made of dark brown wood, but with all the scratches that showed a lighter variety of colors within, it looked sandy brown. It was rickety and worn, but despite all this, the 2 boys were proud of it. After all, it was their boat. They had bought it with their own pocket money from the old man who sat beneath the sun most of the day with a cigar in his hand. They had imagined for a long time, how fun it would be if they could go sailing on their own. And when they saw the vehicle slowly blackening in the sun one day, they asked the old man if they could buy it. It was already a couple of years old when they first saw it at the beach, so he gave it to them for a cheap price.

They had to hide it from their parents and family members for fear of a scolding, but that was taken care of by a snug nook they had found while roaming about. Its bushes and creepers could easily hide the vehicle. But only one boy could get the hang of driving the watercraft. Coincidentally, he had been named 'Noah', which brought forth regular puns and teasing from the other boy and his best friend, George. Now they had been floating peacefully towards nowhere when George took out the Swiss army knife from his pocket. It had been a present from his father, a trader, who had come home for the first time in a couple of years. He had bought the multi-use tool during his stay in Switzerland. He had brought George more gifts, but this one was George's most favorites.

'Wish I could have one, myself' Noah said, looking at the instrument which now betrayed its workings within due to the late afternoon sun. A cold fire of jealousy ignited in his heart, and he had a strong desire to possess the instrument.

'Isn't it just brilliant?' George said. 'The handle is made of a rare type of glass, and the tools inside are made with high-quality steel. Father said it himself. I bet it is worth a pretty penny, anytime.'

'Can't argue with that. Say what, how about 12 ice lollies for that thing. No, make that 15'

'I'm sorry captain, but the answer for that would be a flat 'no'. And anyway, dad would probably kill me if I gave it to anyone. You don't want to see him when he goes full-on-rage, I'm telling you.

'Can't go against that either. I daresay most fathers aren't like that.' Noah said, a little disappointed. 'Anyway, did you hear about

Liverpool winning the first division for the 12th time? One of my cousins went to .....'

The talk slowly diverged away from the palm-sized tool into other happenings of interest.

It wasn't after half an hour that the pair of boys noticed the tide rising a little, and decided to head back to the coast. At about 3:45, they were almost on the sandy lands, when the boys had a stroke of bad luck.

'Noah!' George cried out.'Mate, watch out!'

But it was too late. They had lost themselves in their world of fantasies, and they paid the price. The 3-foot high wave crashed into their vehicle, and due to the boat's lack of quality and the lack of balance, it toppled over, pushing the two children into the water. Fortunately, both were strong swimmers. Naturally, you couldn't be a bad one if you lived near the coast. The wave did not have much force, so they didn't find themselves too deep beneath the surface when they started kicking their legs and propelling themselves up.

They swam towards the shore. They weren't concerned about the boat, and they were right not to be. A few moments later, A wave similar to the one that had crashed into them, deposited it near them. The 2 children ran over to it and quickly pulled it over to the sand to save it from the retreating water.

'That was quite a dive we had there.' Noah said, as he squinted and blinked at a rapid pace due to the salt water, simultaneously helping George to upright the watercraft. 'Yeah.' George said as he rubbed his eyes using one of his hands covered with salt water. Then he moaned. 'Ah! I forgot my hand had taken the dive too.'

The 2 were just going to hide the boat in their cave, when Noah realized something.'The ocean took the oar.' Noah complained. 'That thing was almost new and about a fourth of the boat's price. Now we'll have to buy another one'

'You'll have to pay 3/5th of the cost. After all, It was due to your carelessness that we lost it.' George said accusingly.

'Hey! That's not fair. Even you could have seen the wa...' Noah stopped short as he saw the sly grin on his friend's face. He gave a playful shove.

Now that the boat was upright and safely stowed away from prying eyes, the pair took their slippers which they had put in a corner and started towards the mainland.

But unlike the boys normally expected, all did not go well. The adventure hadn't yet finished. In fact, a new adventure had begun. An adventure that would take a couple of decades to finish. While they were mid-way, Noah had a thought. A thought that sent horror creeping into George.

'By the way, speaking of the ocean stealing things, you still have that pocket knife, don't you?'

George stopped mid-stride. His brain slowly extended its senses into his right thigh- the place, where an hour before, a cool and heavy object had rested. Now, that weight was absent.

George's head spun. It felt heavy, and he felt dizzy. His whole body turned hot, forcing him to experience the atmosphere around him in a colder and harsher way. He sat down on a nearby rock, unable to stand.

Noah sighed. He understood what had happened even though his companion hadn't uttered a word. It was obvious. He shook his head, his face morphing into a sad expression. However, deep inside him, the cold fire of jealousy stopped burning. He felt a sense of satisfaction. He hated himself to the high heavens for feeling such a way, but one couldn't stop feelings. He hadn't stolen it. Oh no! He wouldn't steal anything, for the fear of a guilty conscience. But his soul silently thanked the wave which had caused this issue.

'It's fine mate.' he said, trying to reassure the figure who had been a jovial boy, but was now a grave-faced and pale being.

'What will I tell my father?' George croaked. He bit his lip, the sign that he was deep in thought. But this time, he bit harder. Blood seeped out, but George hardly felt it.

'We'll figure something out. Don't worry too much.' Noah said ' I've heard something from my dad once: For everything that happens in this universe, there is a reason, a good one. He heard it from a monk'

George turned with a cynical expression on his face. 'Are you serious?'

A smile tugged at Noah's lips and he shrugged. 'For all you know, that blade you lost could save a life!'

Part II

-19 Years later-

Footsteps thudded along the area near the coast. Two pairs of legs, both wearing pants, and flexible shoes, ran like the wind, one pair chasing the other. Each footfall displaced wet, damp sand from its original position and caused minuscule ripples in the nearby puddles of water.

The owner of the pair of legs that succeeded the other was a dashing man, presumably in his mid-thirties. He had a sharp chin, flat cheeks, and piercing dark blue eyes that scouted his surroundings for anything that would prove advantageous in his given circumstances. His body was a muscular, well-toned one- all the signs of a good agent.

He ran in zig-zag lines, a simple tactic for dodging bullets, while his chaser ran in a straight line, trying to aim with his gun. Though his body was covered with sweat, his willpower was enough to keep him going; admirable for a man who had a couple of bullets lodged in his left wrist and arm, and one on his left shoulder. The man recalled that shot. He had somehow sensed the bullet coming in at the last millisecond. He couldn't drop down to avoid the shot completely. All that would have done was get him a piece of metal in his brain. Also, dropping down would have required him to get up again, and he couldn't have mustered enough strength to do that quickly. Therefore, to stop the bullet from entering his subclavian artery, it proved necessary to intercept its path with his arm. So, he had taken the shot in his left arm, as his left wrist was already not of any use.

However, with each bad moment, comes a good one.

'Just 2 more rounds' he thought.

The Glock 18 pistol that his opponent held had the capacity to hold....... well, 18 bullets. He had been silently counting down on the gun's capacity, and not to his surprise, each bullet wasted had made the next one more accurately shot.

The man turned his gaze to his left, and a jolt of pain almost made him lose his footing. But afterward, his eyes slowly turned sideways to look at a path - one which led to a small cave. The cave which probably still housed his and his friend's boat. 'Noah. Where would he be right now?' he thought.

George hadn't seen his friend from the day they had parted ways. George's interest had gone towards the army while Noah had wanted to go to the marine industry.

'No.' George thought. There will be much time for thinking about old friends tomorrow- if he would ever have one. He had to think of a way to escape from this situation now.

George had been very interested in the foreign intelligence agency, and after 5 years of vigorous training, he had finally attained a position for himself in the M16. All that seemed like decades before. All that sweat, and blood he had given to reach this position- all that would go to waste if he did not survive this chase scene.

The man chasing him was a criminal mastermind, one who had killed hundreds and would kill hundreds more. George, and 5 more soldiers were sent to capture the man they had been chasing for more than a decade now. The intelligence office had found the place he was living at. It was in a village. George's heart had skipped a beat when he had asked the exact location.

'Polperro sir.' came the reply. It was the reason he had been selected. He knew the layout of the area better than anyone else.

The mission was scheduled for the afternoon, as the bustling area at that time would decrease the chances of the crime lord escaping. A few causalities were the least of their problems compared to the hundreds the criminal had killed. A couple of dozen policemen could just barge into the location and secure the area. But, the scoundrel would have fled by then. What they needed was a few undercover agents in action.

So that was what was done. 6 agents were sent, and George had led them. Everything had been going fine until suddenly 15 men armed with rifles dropped from the upper floors of the abandoned old building they had been in.

At that time, each member of the small task force sent in had experienced slight fear. Someone had sold them out. But they soon recovered. After all, that was what they had been trained to do. George, knowing that jammers would soon be turned on, had swiftly taken his walkie-talkie in his hands, and had sent a quick message. He had barely finished when the jammers came into effect and the signal got cut.

The main entrance of the building had been blocked, so there was no means of escape there, but George had remembered something which gave him a spark of hope. There was a thin staircase exactly beside the place in which they had been cornered- a staircase which was a part of a restaurant. The restaurant had two levels, and one could enter or exit the building from the restaurant's second level also. Therefore, if George ran up the staircase, he could escape from the 2nd level's exit. George's mind had thought all of this in a few brief moments. By the time George had formulated his plan, the fifteen men had still not formed a perfect containment formation around the six agents. There had still been a few holes in their formation, and coincidentally, one of those holes had provided a direct passage to the narrow staircase. George had exploited this fact and had made a run for it, not looking back.

There had been a few shouts of frustration from his opponents, sounds of bullet shots, and that of footsteps. However, the majority of the footsteps were thudding away from him. With this, he had known that his comrades had taken his attempt to escape as a distraction and had started moving themselves.

But as for that moment, luck had not been on his side. In the second level, he had found himself face to face with four more men with rippling muscles, of which two had held a gun. What ensued then, was a series of cat and mouse chases across floors of the building, in which George had emptied all his resources just to stay alive. There, he had obtained his shot in the wrist.

Thankfully, the probability of him getting a shot in his leg had been low as most of his fights had taken place in the upper levels of the building, which had barricades in the corridors that overlooked the floors below. So, when an opponent shot his gun from the corridor opposite George's corridor, George's legs were protected by the barricades.

He had then somehow reached a room that had been a kitchen when the building had thrived once. He had expected it to be empty and had hoped that he could catch his breath there. Instead, he found himself face to face with the great crime lord, he and his team had been looking for.

They stared at each other for a few seconds, but it had felt like an eternity to George.

George made the first move, and he ran. Not towards the door, but in the direction of the man responsible for his presence there.

The man had scrambled for his gun, and that was where George had gotten his second shot in his arm.

But after all that, George hadn't tried to attack the criminal. Under circumstances in which he'd had a gun or even a knife, he would have, but now he was blank. He had spent all his ammunition in killing 3 of the men he had seen on the stairs and escaping the last one. He had run and crashed into the window behind his opponent. He had landed on the ground running and his opponent had followed behind. He had not called his goons who would have taken more than two minutes to even reach this location unlike what one sees in the movies.

Both men had run with no recognition of the paths they took, getting them where they are now.

And so that was how George had ended up being chased by a man with a pistol. But thankfully, all the training he had done had worked out, and he was still alive.

He still had hope.

The man chasing him was still running, instead of stopping to aim. With good reason. They were running in a busy area. Not surrounded by people, but by trees and rocks. It was easy to hide among them, and hence was a great place to practice guerrilla tactics.

But George's luck ran out. Again. The cover stopped and he broke out into the beach. That was all George could manage. The continuous disappointments erased the thought of hope from his mind. His shoulders drooped as he gave up. Sensing victory, his opponent fired, and a bullet went right into George's right thigh.

Blood flowed. George slowed. his feet collided with a rock sticking out of the ground and all the momentum he had built up was used to throw him in a straight path through the air. He flipped twice, before he hit the ground, buttocks first. He slowly sat up and pulled himself towards a big boulder, and supported his backbone over its smooth surface.

He was going to die anyway. Why not die in a comfortable state? He took in the fresh sea air. The same air he had breathed in his childhood. He would die in the same land where he had been born. His oppressor jogged towards him to a stop. His breath, in contrast to George's, was just a little strained, showing off his stamina. He smirked.

'Not so proud of your decision to support the law now are you, Mr. George?

In spite, of his depression, George's mind exploded with realizations and questions.'You know my name.' He said. 'How? Why? Who told you all this? Who told you we would be coming here today?

The crime lord smiled. 'Oh, I have my ways. But you didn't possibly think I would tell you, did you?'

'It was worth the try.' the reply was croaked out with difficulty.

'Maybe. But even if I did say, you wouldn't be alive to talk about it.'

George shuddered. It was one to read about death in books. It was another to face it.

'If you're going to kill me, just do it fast.'

'Oh no, dear lad, why would I do that?' The man who was now intently looking down at him cried. 'You are a potential source of information for me to exploit, you being the leader of the force that intruded into my humble abode and what not.'

George's mind reeled. He had wondered why the first 2 bullets had not hit his neck or head- if bullets had been shot there, he would have been killed instantly. He had presumed that the shooters responsible for those shots had just been improperly trained. But now he understood. The criminal's objective was not to kill him but to capture him. His heart trembled as he wondered what had happened to his fellow agents. But he didn't express those thoughts.

'Hardly humble.' George mumbled. 'I won't open my mouth even if you roast me. For all I am of use to you, you could just kill me.'

'Oh, rea -'

The man was cut off as a great wave slammed into them with a roar. It had been creeping upon them and both men had failed to notice it, and had paid the price.

When it retreated, George was dripping wet while the other just had his pants full of salt water. After all, George had been sitting while the other wasn't.

Saltwater dripped from his eyebrows. But George didn't care. Not because he was going to die, but because he was going to live. The great wave had deposited something exactly in the space present between his lower back and the boulder he had been resting on. It was exactly in George's oppressor's blind spot. His right arm, which had been near to the place the object rested, took the object it and felt it. He ran his thumb across one of its surfaces. When he did, it stung like hell. George cried out. 'Ah!'

The enemy, sensing something was wrong, instantly raised his arm and fired.

George, sensing his opportunity to live slipping away, threw the object in his hands with a swift arc of his right arm. A gleaming blade, with a thick handle of a deep turquoise blue, flew at the other man like a stroke of lightning.

For a moment, luck favored George. The bullet that came at him went straight towards his chest. It went with such speed that George's eyes couldn't have tracked it, but even if he had, he wouldn't have panicked.

After all, he was wearing body armor. The bullet slammed with a force that had been enhanced more than ever due to the pistol's close proximity, but nevertheless, it couldn't penetrate the bulletproof cloth.

But that moment of luck came to an end. George's heart sank as he saw that he had not aimed properly. The knife would go just above the intended target's head.

He closed his eyes.

He prepared to die.

But to his surprise, he heard a strangled cry. That cry slowly turned into a gurgle. George opened his eyes in surprise. The knife had gone straight through the crime lord's throat, cutting off his air pipe. Blood spurted out, and his body went still.

The knife was not a normal one. It was a swiss knife. It was a collection of multiple tools. So, it was a lot heavier than any knife George had thrown. So, even though George threw it a little higher than he had intended to , the additional weight pulled it down, making it land where it was intended to

George's head fell back and he heaved a great sigh. He had done it.

Part III

Exactly 2 Years later. Time: 3:44

George floated in a boat near the Polperro beach, remembering the events that had happened a couple of years earlier.

He held his savior. The knife. It was a vibrant blue-colored swiss knife. It had Switzerland's flag's symbol on it - a white-colored plus sign surrounded by a red-colored rectangle. The rest of it was, to speak precisely, a shade of deep and translucent turquoise blue, coincidentally the same color as the sea around him.

George laughed.

'You were right Noah.' He said to no one in particular. 'Only it didn't save *a* life. It saved many. And now, it must save more.' saying this, he dropped the knife into the sea.

&

George had checked his watch right after the knife had gone through his enemy's throat.

It had been 3:45

&

III

Green fingers

It was a pleasant evening and the light orange hue of the recently sunken afternoon sun hovered about in the sky. Jack Bryans stood in front of the local supermarket; a slender hand pushed inside his tiny left shorts pocket and his face was partially covered by shadow due to his hood. He wore neon-colored shorts with small pockets, a T-shirt with a baggy orange jacket on top, and Nike shoes. He liked to wear trousers and t-shirts - they did not stick to your body like a second skin all the time - like those annoying jeans. But at the same time, he did not like wearing anything with small pockets or wearing a jacket on a summer day, either. But, he did not have any choices for those two. Though not essential in the job he was about to do, they would help him in a few ways.

One might think- 'why would anyone want small pockets and jackets for shopping?' But Jack was not about to do shopping. He was going to **steal**.

Jack Bryans was not a starved or badly brought-up boy. But, at some point of time, he got bored of normal life and decided that he wanted some action. After a few gangster movies and the first 3 Artemis fowl books, he resolved to become a criminal mastermind.

Quite a far-fetched idea for a 13-year-old, don't you think?

But Jack was determined to stick to it. But he reasoned that he could not just go and steal diamonds. He needed to have some practice. So he started stealing small things, like chocolates, and candy.

He loved the thrill of the few moments when he was inside the shop with the adventurous objective. He loved the thought of outwitting someone. And the free candy did not hurt either.

But also, stealing is not as easy as it sounds. You cannot just enter a shop, grab a couple of candy bars and barge out of the place. No, there would be about 20 people working there and you would need to be very careful. Also, Jack did not like leaving any traces around. According to him, only if not even a slight thought of suspicion had entered any one of the staffs' minds, it was a job well done. That was why Jack had his own set of tricks: - tricks that had been built up with months of experience.

'Time to put step 1 into action' He thought.

Jack started jogging around the supermarket. After a couple of rounds, he entered the supermarket, now at a normal pace. The sliding door moved aside with a soft 'click' and Jack entered removing his hood- not breathing heavily, but not breathing at the normal pace either. If a stranger looked at him, he would probably deduce that the boy had run to reach his destination just like all common and hyperactive boys-just what Jack wanted people to believe. If he had just walked in slowly, without any 'heavy breathing', it would not produce a big effect, but when one sees a boy looking at a supermarket thoughtfully and entering in slowly, it might look strange.

Jack entered the supermarket with a confident air and took a deep breath when inside the building as cool air produced by the air conditioner hit him like a tidal wave.

'Good evening' he called out to the lady behind the checking counter. The lady smiled and greeted him back with a slight bow. Another one of Jack's Rules-Never show that you are stressed/ going to do something unlikable, although Jack had so much experience that he did not even think about his next move, leave alone the thought of being stressed.

Next, pretending that he did not do it on purpose, he would now give his leg a little kick that no naked eye could see- and the clink of two coins slapping together would ring out. This would give the impression that he had money to spend, but in reality, he had 2 dirhams only. But this time, perhaps in overconfidence, he gave a little more force by mistake. If someone had had quick eyes, they would have been able to realize this boy had kicked purposefully. Jack flinched. He tensed and looked around to see if anyone had seen- his eyes darting like a wild predator. With relief, he noticed that the little customers present were counting their money or doing their job. A slight smile tugged at his face as his quick eyes noticed the slight perk of the counter's ears due to the clap of the coins, but he did not show it.

He had just taken a step towards the stationery- and the chocolate section when he noticed something else. Or more specifically, he felt something. He looked up and just there, at the entrance to the aisle where he had been heading, a man was standing, staring straight at him. He wore a dim multicolored shirt, which effectively camouflaged him with his surroundings. He was opening a box of newly arrived pens and markers and was in the act of testing a few green markers on his fingernails and then, stacking them on the shelves neatly. He had apparently been testing many such boxes since almost all his fingers, not just the nails, had already become green.

'A new recruit!' thought Jack 'he still doesn't have his uniform.'

Jack made eye contact and took an uncertain step forward.

He still intended to go with the plan, but just seeing the man's face made him shiver. It was not his features, but his stare- It seemed to penetrate Jack's skull and read his thoughts.

Thankfully, the man shifted his gaze and went on with his work. Jack scolded himself for not being in control of his emotions and went on with his work, but more cautiously now, as he knew that curiosity or suspicion (probably the latter) had entered the mind of at least one person here.

Jack could have just fled the scene muttering some excuse, but he did not do that. He liked challenges and if he did walk away without buying anything, the man's suspicions would be confirmed and the next time Jack entered the supermarket, he may try to talk to him. The boy in orange walked up to the stationary section, passed the man, and started inspecting a few gel pens, right next to him. Out of the corners of his eyes, he could see the man trying to keep an eye on him through the corners of his eyes.

Jack knelt to inspect a few books. He flipped a few pages and then pretending that something else had caught his attention, he walked to his left and kneeled just at the edge of the stationary section, where the candy section began. He took out a leather-bound black book and started examining it.

Giving the impression that he liked the book and intended to buy it, he took the book in his arms and rose. At that moment, he pretended that he had just seen the chocolates, and went over and looked at the candy-like how normally any kid would do. He acted so perfectly and gave the perfect expressions that, suspicion and hostility would not have a chance to enter one's mind unless someone already knew what was going on and tried to relate things.

Jack selected a bar of candy and holding both the objects in his hands, walked out of the aisle. But while he passed the man, he stole a quick glance at the box the man was taking and stacking the markers from. This was very important - if the man still had markers to stack, Jack would not be able to steal a few things with the scary man beside him. Fortunately, Jack noticed with relief that the markers were already finished, and the man was just erecting a few of the toppled-over pens.

Perhaps as an excuse to keep an eye on him?

He walked up to the counter and asked the price of the 2 things he had in his hands. The receptionist first scanned the bar of candy and voiced out its price. Jack nodded, showing he was satisfied. The receptionist took the scanner in her hand and started scanning the black book. Out of the corner of his eyes, Jack noticed with satisfaction that the man had tossed the now empty box aside, taken a bottle of cleaning spray, and was heading towards the magazine stand near the exit. Perhaps thinking that the boy was going to go and maybe he was after all, innocent.

The receptionist finished scanning the book and handed it to Jack simultaneously stating the price. Jack pretended to show displeasure at the costly price. Although this time the price really was high, even if the price were right, Jack would not have bought it. The book was just a distraction. He made a show of hiding his fake disappointment and told the receptionist that he would just be buying the candy and went into the stationery aisle to return the book to its place.

At normal times, he would not have bought even that small candy, but he wanted to show the man that he was buying something. But he decided to still stick to the plan. He could not bear losing his candy because of a slight suspicion.

He walked up to the aisle at a normal pace but just after he was out of eyesight, he quickened his pace, almost running towards the candy section. As he reached its edge, he stuffed the book into one of the neatly stacked shelves and unzipped his jacket. Then he quickly selected a few fine bars of chocolate, took them in his hand, and placed each one of them neatly inside a hidden pocket on the inner sides of his jacket. He made sure to take only candy bars and not things like chocolate eggs which would bulge out of his pocket, while bars were flat and would be easy to conceal.

He was about to go back to the counter when his eyes caught on a gleaming bar of chocolate. Jack's eyes shot up. That was a Godiva candy bar and very expensive. He loved its taste, but they were usually sold out every time within about an hour of their arrival. Jack took the bar in his hand and stared at it.

No matter what, he must have it.

If he had paid closer attention, he would have noticed that the bar was covered by a smooth aluminum foil underneath the cover and would have put it back. But he quickly put the bar into his jacket and zipped it up.

A fatal Mistake.

He looked down at his jacket. There was not a trace of anything he had put in there.

He then walked up confidently to the counter and took out his 2 coins to pay for the bar of candy. He saw the receptionist's eyes dart to his pockets to see if he had taken anything. This was where the small pockets came in. Jack's phone was tucked in his left pocket. But because of the pocket's size, half of the phone stuck out. The lady caught sight of this and immediately concluded that the boy had not taken anything as his pockets were so small. And as for the jacket, jackets did not have pockets, did they?

A smile tugged at Jack's face. 'If only she knew!'

Jack took the bar, stuffed it into his pocket, and headed for the exit. 'At last!' thought Jack. Another job well done!

But it seemed that fate had other plans for the thief, for, at that precise moment when he passed the man who was still cleaning the magazine stand, a rustling sound came from the inside of Jack's pocket.

Jack wanted to hit himself in the face. Why had not he thought of it! Chocolates covered with a smooth aluminum foil gave out a rustling sound when one moved with it! And the Godiva bar had been covered with a foil!

Involuntarily, he quickened his pace and wished with all his heart that the man had not heard the sound. He slowed down a bit as he went a little further from the shop. He tried to reassure himself that the man might not have heard the rustle as he had been completely absorbed in his work. Or had he pretended?

He did not turn around to confirm this himself. He had a nagging feeling that prevented him from doing so. Also, he knew that if his assumptions were true and he saw the man behind him, he would instinctively run. That would land him in trouble. But Jack's confidence grew with every step he took away from the store – with every step away from the man.

He was just about to completely believe that he had hit a stroke of luck and open a candy bar to celebrate when he froze. Someone had placed something on his shoulder.

It was a hand. A rough hand. A hand with green fingers.

IV
Hello, Cerebrum Speaking!

'Yes mom, I've been eating well, might have even put on a few more pounds. But no, I am not lonely. Made some friends. I am not an amateur in that area, thank gods.'

An electronic feminine voice rang out from the computer in front of the boy who had spoken,' Pounds! Pounds you say? Where did the poor 'kilos' go to? Ah, just a few weeks in the US and you're speaking like you were born there!' the voice chuckled. 'Anyway, it doesn't matter. I hope you are comfortable. I thought they served nothing other than burgers and french fries. If it was me who was going to college, I would choose a place where they serve rice and chapatis.

Rajeev smiled. 'No mom. They don't serve only that. There's mashed potatoes, baked chicken, and the normal cafeteria-style dishes. Also, I like western food. So, there is no problem. Don't fret. I have my classes now. I'll call you later. OK?

The figure on the google meet screen frowned and looked at the wall clock hung behind her.

'But it is afternoon now. Your classes start-. Oh! The time lag'. 'Sure dear, fine. I will WhatsApp you if your father comes. Just speak with him if possible.'

Rajeev was going to cut the call when his mother spoke again.

'Wait! I just remembered. How are you sleeping?'

That question bought forth an impish grin on Rajeev's face.

'Well,....'

'Well, what? It's been troubling you again hasn't it?

'Yes,' the reply was hesitant.

'How many classes were you absent for?

'6'

Rajeev's problem was this. *Sleep.* Not the lack of it, but an excess of it. When he started sleeping, no one could wake him up. A wrecking ball could have demolished his house, and he would have probably stirred a little.

This problem was such an intense one that once, he missed his 9th-grade maths exam because he had slept in the bathroom when he was having a bath in the morning. His mother had woken him up with a slap, but his sleepiness had settled in again in the shower. His mother, blissfully unaware of her son's state, had gone back to sleep, completely exhausted after working in the kitchen for a long time. She had thought that he would have grown up by then and would have caught the bus. It was only after 2 hours that he was discovered, slightly drooling.

After that incident, he had been put on strict training by his father for sleeping lightly. Slowly he improved, but then came college. A place where infinite freedom was given. He was sent to the USA under the thought that he would gain more exposure to the world.

But that had just worsened his habits.

'Did you try the loud alarm clock I gave you when you were packing?'

'Yes, mom. It was the first thing I did. It worked for a day, but then.... I think I just adapted.' Rajeev's mother sighed.

'Then I can't do anything. Sorry, but that will be your bridge to cross. All I can say is just before you sleep concentrate very hard, and think with all your willpower that you have to wake up, and so you shall. Our subconscious mind is a very powerful thing dear. Sometimes, it may even try to communicate with us to make our lives easier!'

Rajeev smiled. 'Sure mother, I will do that. I daresay it will work though.'

And with that, the call was cut.

తు

That night, Rajeev was about to go to sleep, when he remembered what his mother said.

He snorted. Concentration it seemed. *The previous generation and its beliefs.* How would his brain send a message to his body to voluntarily wake up when he was asleep?

'Nevertheless, I should try it' he thought. 'I have nothing to lose.'

With that, he closed his eyes, sat in a meditative pose, and concentrated as hard as he could, saying the same chant over and over again in his mind- Have to wake up at 8 AM, Have to wake up at 8 AM, Have to wake up at 8 AM, Have to wake up at 8 AM....

After a few minutes, he slowly opened his eyes. Nothing felt different. He giggled, shook his head, spread his blanket over himself, and dozed off with the thought - *Damn, it's cold.*

తు

The next morning, Rajeev woke up with a start. What a strange dream he had experienced! It was a dream with clocks, cats, ice creams, and bloody knives. He couldn't remember exactly was it was though, just like all dreams.

And then he felt something about him that he felt different. He frowned.

And then he got it. He felt fresh. He didn't feel sleepy. He did not feel as if he wanted to go back to sleep again. And then his eyes landed on the clock. It was exactly 7:59 AM.

The whole day his mind kept drifting back to that same incident. How had that happened? It surely wasn't supernatural! Rajeev didn't believe in all those things, but now he doubted himself. His mind drifted towards what his mother had said. The 6th time in the last 24 hours.

'Our subconscious mind is a very powerful thing dear' she had said.

Could that be true? But then he had already tried out that exercise when he had been younger. It didn't work then, why should it work now? He compared both his younger self's and his phenomenons. The difference was that at that time, his stakes were low, but now, he could lose a lot if he lost a day due to sleep.

The whole thing still sounded strange to him. Very strange.

'Well' he thought 'the only way to find a solution for a problem is to experiment

And so he did. He tried to wake up at different times: like 7 AM, or 8:30 AM. It worked.

Only when he tried to wake up very early: like 5 AM, would it become a little difficult. He would wake up, only to fall asleep again.

But the strange thing was that he experienced the same dream: the one about clocks, cats, ice creams, and bloody knives every day. But each day, right after he woke up, he would slowly start to forget the dream. So he made another plan: right after he woke up, he would take a pocket notebook and write down what he remembered.

A week later, he had a basic outline of the dream. Sometimes he would remember one aspect of his dream, like the detailed account of the part in which he would see cats or ice creams. Sometimes he would experience nothing and wouldn't have anything to write in his notebook that day.

A couple of weeks later, he had a detailed account of the dream jotted down in neat handwriting in his pocket diary.

He looked with satisfaction at the text. He knew what his next step was clear. He knew that this dream would have something to do with his strange suddenly developed habit of waking early. He would have to find out the meaning of the dream.

When one needs the meaning of a word, he looks it up in a dictionary.

When one needs the meaning of a dream, he looks it up in a dream interpreter.

So that's what Rajeev did. Within minutes, he was on an online website dedicated to interpreting dreams. With moderate speed, he typed out the words he had written in his pocket diary, copying them correctly, so as to not make any mistakes.

When he had finished, he pressed enter with a trembling finger.

A new window opened.

Rajeev's eyes widened in anxiousness.

The window loaded and came into full view.

Rajeev read the text written on the screen.

Then he read it again.

Then he roared with laughter. Tears of amusement wet his eyes and he raised his face towards the sky, which's view was blocked by the ceiling. 'Mother, mother, mother,' He said to no one in particular. 'You told me that "Sometimes, our subconscious mind may even try to communicate with us to make our lives easier!"'. 'Well guess what. I understood what my mind was trying to say to me. I am sure i don't know if my subconscious mind is a powerful thing, but it sure is downright rude!

The cause for all this was, (as you might have guessed), what was written on the screen of Rajeev's computer. The text written there was just 4 simple words.

WAKE UP, YOU DIMWIT!

V
The Art of Forgetting

I am forgetful

Those 3 words are the simplest that can be used to describe me, for if I were to elaborate, time would run like the wind.

Reasons fly beyond my reach, but how much ever I try to remember something, I forget it. In fact, you could say that the more I try to remember something, the more easily I forget it.

Even my nickname had been 'Goldfish' which everyone thought had a memory of 3 seconds. (But now it is proven that they can remember a maximum of 5 months! So there!). Examples that exist of my personality are extremely ridiculous. There are some incidents that are so intricate in their details that one choice changes everything. Although absent-minded, I pride myself on having an extremely artistic and logical mind, for that combination, seems to me a strange mix.

Once, I was doing a small experiment to find answers for a 'not so difficult to find' question in my mind. It is always a principle of mine to not seek information from the internet unless and until there is no other way, or I fail to seek it by myself. This also serves as an excuse to not study subjects that were unfortunate enough to not gain my favor.

Here, the question was: What was the substance that kept the ink in a ball pen from flowing out through the open side of the ink chamber?

To gain the answer to that question, I took a red ball pen and a hairpin. I unscrewed the back of the pen but didn't take the thin ink chamber out (for the fear of forgetting to replace it back). I poked the hairpin into the thin tube in the pen which contained the dark and concentrated red fluid. However, I could see that it was too short and didn't reach the end of the ink. Hence I abandoned the thin piece of sharp metal and went in search of a different instrument that would help me obtain my answers.

After continuous searching, I found a metal paper clip which I managed to straighten out. I poked my customized metal stick into the ink tube. On pulling it out, I found a transparent, near-invisible gel stuck to its tip. Upon research, I found that it was a type of grease called 'stopper fluid' which helped to stop the ink from flowing out and evaporating.

I also learned that removing it from a pen's ink chamber could give birth to disaster. Therefore, before I showed it to my brother and mother, I made a mental note to put the gel back into the pen afterward.

You might have already guessed, but I immediately forgot about it.

What I expected from my mother when I showed her my discovery was a smile and a 'good work'.

What I didn't expect was what I heard from her - a line of words that gave the message, 'Stop wasting time' (albeit in a harsh way) and a reminder that I had my online tuition in 5 minutes.

Ouch.

Now disaster started. It could have been any pen. My brother had been playing with 5 of them. There were half a dozen in the spare box, and our dog Mutt (Don't ask how he got his name. It is a long story) was burying a couple in his sandbox as an addition to the unknown horrors that already lay buried in there.

But no. It had to be the subject of my activity. As I waited for my teacher, I 'absent-mindedly' sucked the back of my pen. I felt a bitter taste in my mouth but ignored it.

After 15 minutes of waiting, I threw my pen down in frustration and went to get a can of soda.

On returning, the sight that caught my eyes filled me with dread. My pen, which was lying on the top of my new hard-bound notebook, had emptied its chambers upon the open pages of my notebook. In my hurry to clean up the mess and to think of an excuse to convince my mother when she saw the notebook, I dropped my pen stand, shattering the glass cup into a thousand pieces. This drew upon the attention of my mother, who came running in and asked me what in the world had just happened here.

Then something queer happened. I opened my mouth to spit out a few words I had readied for myself, and my mother screamed.

Huh?

It should have actually been the other way round, for, without her hairband, my mother's hair springs up making her look like Medusa.

The next few seconds are a blur to me now, but I remember my mother forcing open my jaw and squinting. Also, she slipped on some ink and hurt her back .I also remember her yelling at me to 'look at a mirror for heaven's sake!'.

Well, I did just that and, when opening my mouth, discovered that I had gotten a brilliant streak of rosy red from the back of my tongue to its tip. My mother had freaked out when she had seen the 'blood'.

Remembering that reminds me of the story of the mongoose, the mother, the child, and the snake.

Not that I'm a mongoose though.

Anyway, back to the story. You could understand the little relief that I felt when I knew that I no longer needed to show my face in my tuition.

Online learning saves the day!

Until ma'am asks me to turn on the camera.

Ugh.

Many a time my forgetfulness has led to losing favor and trust among people. For example, you ask?

Well then, Example: My Mother!

And to give my mother some credit, she is quite tolerating and a fast forgiving person.

Anyway, the incident started like this:

It had just been my 10th birthday, and boy! Was I excited to enter into the double digits! I started 'carrying myself like a man ought to' and started thinking that I had become responsible due to the simple fact that I had become 10.

Now, I had been attending art classes. At the end of every month, my father came with me to pay the fees. However, at the end of one November, I persuaded my mother to let me give the fees to my teacher. Reluctantly, my mother pushed a couple of bills into my pant pocket, lecturing me about how much money was in there, how must of it I should give, to whom should I give it, blah, blah, blah, blah, blah, blah, blah, blah. (You can't expect me to remember all that!)

My father came in the middle of our conversation and my mother summarized to him, what was just happening.

His expression could not have portrayed his thoughts more perfectly.

Are you sure?

My mother's was the same.

No.

Thank you for all the confidence you have in me mother!

I packed up my bag and started walking to my class. Just like normal, I started daydreaming. I dream about many things. Like, 'what I am going to learn today',

'how my teacher's expression would be when I show her my latest painting',

'what if a wizard appeared out of thin air and told me that I was invited to study at Hogwarts?'

'Or what if a blue spider hanging from the wall of our driveway dropped down and bit me?'

and so on...

I was just in the middle of an awesome dream about me being a ninja when the art center came into view. I sighed and paused my dream to continue it later.

I entered the center with a smile and wished my teacher good morning.

We started pencil shading that day, and by the time my session was over, I knew most of the kinds of pencil textures there were to know.

I walked out of the center and went home, and started my weekend with a complaint from my mother about how stinky I was and that I should put my clothes into the laundry basket and take a wash.

I did not argue.

At least it gave me a chance to resume the dream of me being a ninja.

ಜ

A day later, my father got a phone call.

The expression on his face was .... indescribable.

He called and asked me if I gave my teacher the fees.

Oops.

I learned afterward that the call had been from the art center asking to 'kindly pay the fees' latest by the day after.

What ensued next, you needn't know in detail. What I can tell you is that a few minutes later, my back was red. But the reason for all this was not about me failing to give the fees, the question was, Where was all the money?

I remember keeping the money in my pant pocket, but which pants had I put on that day? I ran through the small corridor and pushed open the door to the messiest place in the world I called my room.

That was the first time in my whole life, I saw my father smiling and looking at my room. "Thank the gods you don't do your own laundry" He had said.

If anyone had entered the house within the next 45 minutes, they would have been able to steal even our grand piano, for we were extremely focused on finding a pair of my dirty pants.

Sometime later, my mother came home from work holding a bulging bag. Seeing us, she turned on her inquisitive look and my dad explained what had happened. When he finished, she had turned pale.

"Why mother, what happened?" I asked.

She glanced down at the bulging bag she was holding. It was a laundry bag!

It was filled with freshly ironed pants and shirts. Out of all of them though, my eyes caught a glimpse of a pair of yellow shorts, the same which had made me wonder if a ninja could wear bright-colored shorts during his missions.

We found the money. It was in my pocket, just like I had said. But a 50 dirham note was torn and guess what my father did?

Answer: He took back some of my pocket money from my already extremely thin wallet

And to top all these off, there come the smaller disasters which are part of my daily routine.

Here are some I can 'remember'.

- Searching for a fountain pen for 3 hours straight. All while holding it in my hands.
- While searching for a couple of books I find one but not the other. So, I place the first book somewhere and go to find the other. After some time, I find the other. But I forget where I kept the first and start hunting for it again.
- I make my school bag ready for the next day. And then an hour later I forget all that I had done. So, I take out all the books, stationery items, and artifacts thinking it was the supplies I had packed the day before. Then I make my bag again.
- Believe it or not, I once went to a social studies exam thinking it was a science one. You don't need to know how many marks I got in there.

- Going to the supermarket to buy mac and cheese, but forgetting the first word on the way. So I come home with a packet of low-fat mozzarella.

But there are a few advantages too. I am the only one who can repeat the excuse 'I forgot to do my homework madam' (even when I didn't forget about it (miraculously)but was playing on my Play Station the whole day long) and make my teacher believe me.

But now I know what you all are asking. Why not set an alarm clock or something?

Extremely simple answer. I forget to.

Every time I go to set an alarm, I remember some other work to do. And as remembering something is a great luxury for me, I run off to do the work.

Why not ask my parents to set an alarm?

Believe it, I tried it out once, and it worked. For a day. The thing is, I keep forgetting to update my parents on what I need to do that day. So sometimes, an alarm goes off saying:

DO ABC HOMEWORK

21/3/2012

See?

Yesterday I got tired of it and searched the internet for Ways to improve memory.

My search bore fruit and the results were:

1. Chew gum while learning.

I tried it out at school. I did not get any memory power though. I got a pink-colored slip.

2. Move your eyes from side to side.

All that did was make me dizzy.

3. Clench your fists.

The guy seated next to me thought I was a maniac and shifted away from me slightly.

4. Use unusual fonts.

What was that for? To try to make my teacher wear glasses?

5. Doodle.

Now that was easy! The thing was, I was so concentrated on doodling I didn't hear a word that my English teacher said. At least until he tapped me on the shoulder and asked me the meaning of 'floccinaucinihilipilification',
Say what?

6. Laugh.

I don't know about you guys, but when I start an artificial laugh, my stomach gets me a nice and painful constipation.
After that, I quit.
My mother noticed this and asked what happened. I told her everything.
Mistake.
Today she called me and told me to drink a brown thing which she placed on the table. I did't know how it smelled because I didn't go even near it. I asked her what it was and she told me that it was a home-brewed medicine suggested by her friends for more memory power.
I really didn't want to, but she made me drink it. How did it taste? Take the worst medicine you have ever drunk and add it to the taste of a rotten egg. Now multiply that by 50. You still won't be closer to the taste. I had to rinse my mouth an average of 4 times with an extra-strong mint-flavored rinsing concentrate per hour.

For 6 hours. Do the math. But however bad the taste was, I think the brown substance is having an effect on me.

I say this because just now I remembered where I had kept my toothbrush. So, it *maybe* was worth it. My mom is coming toward me holding something in a tray. I'm going to ask her to convey my thanks to her friends. After all, I believe in politeness.

But my words die in my throat as I see what she is carrying in the tray. The medicine!

I start to make a run for it.

See, if this continues, I am going to have to write a new story. '*My mouth stinks...*'

www.ingramcontent.com/pod-product-compliance
Lightning Source LLC
Chambersburg PA
CBHW021146130726
47988CB00004B/1492